Jane Hissey
Hoot

SCRIBBLERS

IT was the middle of the night but Little Bear was wide awake.

'Rabbit,' he whispered, 'I heard a noise.'

'What sort of noise?' muttered Rabbit sleepily.

'A bump,' said Little Bear, 'and then a WhOoOoo. Do you think it's a ghost?'

'Probably just the wind,' said Rabbit.

JUST then a white shape glided past the bed. Rabbit and Little Bear dived under the sheet.

'What was it?' whispered Rabbit.

'I don't know,' said Little Bear.

HE shook Bramwell's paw.

'Wake up!' he whispered. 'Something's making a whoooOo noise.'

'Wind, I expect,' said Bramwell. 'Why are you hiding?'

'We saw it,' said Little Bear. 'But we don't want it to see us!'

NOW all the toys were awake.

'What are you doing?' grumbled Duck. 'It's the middle of the night.'

Then they all heard the noise: Whoooooooo.

Old Bear turned on the bedside light
and reached for his torch.

'I'd better go and see,' he said,
as he set off across the room.

LITTLE Bear and Rabbit looked at their shadows on the wall.

'Let's make scary monsters,' whispered Little Bear, 'to frighten the ghost thing away.'

The monster shadows were looking big and fierce when Old Bear came back.

'I didn't see anything,' he said, 'but the room is much tidier than we left it.'

'Well wind doesn't tidy up,' said Duck.

'A ghost might,' said Little Bear. 'Let's all go and see together.'

THE toys tiptoed across the room. Little Bear held on to Old Bear's paw. Then they heard the noise again. It was right above their heads.

'It's on top of the cupboard!' cried Little Bear.

A̲T that moment something swooped down and landed in front of the toys.
It was a little white owl in a blue apron.

'Hallo,' said the owl. 'What are you doing up in the night? You're usually
fast asleep.'

'WE heard a whooooo noise,' said Little Bear.

'That was me,' said the Owl. 'I'm sorry I woke you up. My name's Hoot.'

'WE heard a bump, too,' said Little Bear.

'That was my nest falling down,' sighed Hoot.

'Oh dear,' said Old Bear. 'Where was your nest?'

'It was up there,' she said, waving a wing at the tall cupboard. 'Only now it's down on the floor.'

'Why haven't we seen you before?' asked Little Bear.

'Owls sleep in the day,' said Hoot, 'and they come out at night when you are asleep. I was always careful not to wake you... until my nest fell down,' she added sadly.

THE toys followed Hoot to the fallen nest.

'It's made of socks!' said Bramwell.

'That's right,' said Hoot. 'I find them all lying around.'

'I wondered where they went!' laughed Bramwell.

'We have a whole drawer full of odd socks!'

'How will you get your nest back up?' asked Rabbit.

'I can't,' said Hoot. 'It just falls apart when I try.'

'I know something that will make a better nest,' cried Little Bear.

HE rushed off and returned with an old woolly bobble hat.

'This won't fall apart,' he said, 'You try it.'

Hoot climbed into the hat and snuggled down.

'Mmm,' she said, 'it's lovely. Thank you. But I don't think I can fly with it.'

'You don't have to,' said Old Bear. He tied a string to the hat and gave the other end to Hoot. 'Now fly up with the string and pull.'

HOOT flew to the top of the cupboard and began to pull the string. As the hat left the ground, Little Bear gave a huge leap and clung to the bobble. The hat slowly rose into the air.

Up and up went Little Bear.

H OOT didn't see him till his ears appeared at the top of the cupboard.

'What are you doing?' she gasped.

'I wanted to see where you lived,' said Little Bear. 'It's very high.'

'It is,' said Hoot, 'and the only way down is to fly.'

'Oh dear,' said Little Bear, 'I hadn't thought of that.'

'Don't worry,' said Hoot, kindly. 'I'll take you down.'

LITTLE Bear climbed onto Hoot's back.

'Hold tight,' she called as she launched herself into the air.

'Look at me!' cried Little Bear, waving to the others. 'I'm flying!'

They flew right round the room then landed next to Old Bear.

'WOULD you like to join me for lunch?' asked Hoot.

'Lunch?' said Little Bear. 'But it's the middle of the night!'

'That's lunchtime for owls!' laughed Hoot. She flew off and returned with a little picnic wrapped in a cloth.

'Mmm, I am quite hungry,' said Little Bear as he shared Hoot's food, 'but I've never had lunch in the middle of the night.'

'TIME for bed now,' said Old Bear, when all the food had gone.

'Thank you, Hoot,' said Little Bear. 'We'll see you another night.'

'And now we know you are asleep in the daytime,' said Rabbit, 'we'll try not to be so noisy!'

Little Bear was so tired, Old Bear had to carry him to bed, and very soon all the toys were fast asleep.

BUT Hoot had a busy night. In the morning all the socks had been sorted into pairs: the ones from Hoot's fallen nest and matching ones from the odd-sock drawer!

THE toys looked up at the cupboard.
'Thank you, Hoot,' they whispered.
They thought they heard a sleepy
whooOooOooOoo,
but it might just have
been the wind
outside.

For Susan, Mark, Laurie and Gina

SALARIYA

www.salariya.com

This edition published in Great Britain in MMXIII by Scribblers, a division of Book House,
an imprint of The Salariya Book Company Ltd
25 Marlborough Place,
Brighton BN1 1UB

www.scribblersbooks.com
www.janehissey.co.uk

First published in Great Britain in MCMXCVI by Hutchinson Children's Books

ISBN-13: 978-1-908973-17-7

3 5 7 9 8 6 4 2

A CIP catalogue record for this book is available from the British Library.

Printed and bound in China
Printed on paper from sustainable sources
Reprinted in MMXIII